W9-AWF-925

THE
ABC
BUNNY

Other Books by Wanda Gág

THE
ABC
BUNNY

By WANDA GA'G
HAND LETTERED BY HOWARD GA'G

University of Minnesota Press
Minneapolis · London

The Fesler-Lampert Minnesota Heritage Book Series

This series reprints significant books that enhance our understanding and appreciation of Minnesota and the Upper Midwest. It is supported by the generous assistance of the John K. and Elsie Lampert Fesler Fund and the interest and contribution of Elizabeth P. Fesler and the late David R. Fesler.

Published by the University of Minnesota Press
111 Third Avenue South, Suite 290
Minneapolis, MN 55401-2520
http://www.upress.umn.edu

Printed in the United States of America on acid-free paper

ISBN 0-8166-4416-0
A Cataloging-in-Publication record for this book is available from the Library of Congress

The University of Minnesota is an equal-opportunity educator and employer.

12 11 10 09 08 07 06 05 04   10 9 8 7 6 5 4 3 2 1

ABC

MUSIC BY FLAVIA GÁG

A for Ap-ple big and red, Tra la la la la la la, B for Bun-n
F for Frog-he's fat and funny, Tra la la la la la la, "Looks like rain," sa

snug a-bed, Tra la la la la la la, C for Crash! D for Dash! E for Elsewher
he to Bun-ny, Tra la la la la la la, G for Gale! H for Hail! Hip-py hop goes

rit.

in a flash Tra la la la la la la la, Elsewhere in a flash, tra la. I for Insec
Bunny's tail Tra la la la la la la la, Hip-py hip-py hop, tra la.

here and there J for Jay with jaunty air K for Kitten catnip-crazy L for Lizar

Look how lazy! M for Meal time— munch, munch, munch! M-m-m! these greens are good for lu

SONG

N for Napping in a nook, O for Owl with bookish look. P for prickly Porc-u-pine
T for Tripping back to Town

Tra la la la la la la, Pins and needles on his spine, Tra la la la la la la
Tra la la la la la la, U for Up and Up-side-down, Tra la la la la la la

Q for Quail, R for Rail, S for Squirrel Swishy-tail, Tra la la la
V for View, Val-ley too, W —— "We welcome you!" Tra la la la

la la la, Squirrel Swishy-tail tra la. X for eXit— off, away!
la la la, Welcome you, tra la tra la.

That's enough for us to-day, Y for You, take one last look, Z for Zero— close the book!

for Apple, big and red

B

for Bunny snug a-bed

C for Crash!

D for Dash!

E

for Elsewhere in a flash

F

for Frog – he's fat and funny

"Looks like rain," says he to Bunny

G for Gale!

H for Hail!

Hippy-hop goes Bunny's tail

I

for Insects here and there

J

for Jay with jaunty air

K

for Kitten , catnip-crazy

L

for Lizard – look how lazy

M

for Mealtime – munch , munch , munch

M-m-m! these greens are good for lunch

N

for Napping in a Nook

O

for Owl with bookish look

P

for prickly Porcupine

Pins and needles on his spine

Q for Quail
R for Rail

S

for Squirrel Swishy-tail

T

for Tripping back to Town

U

for Up and Up-side-down

V for View

Valley too

W

—"We welcome you!"

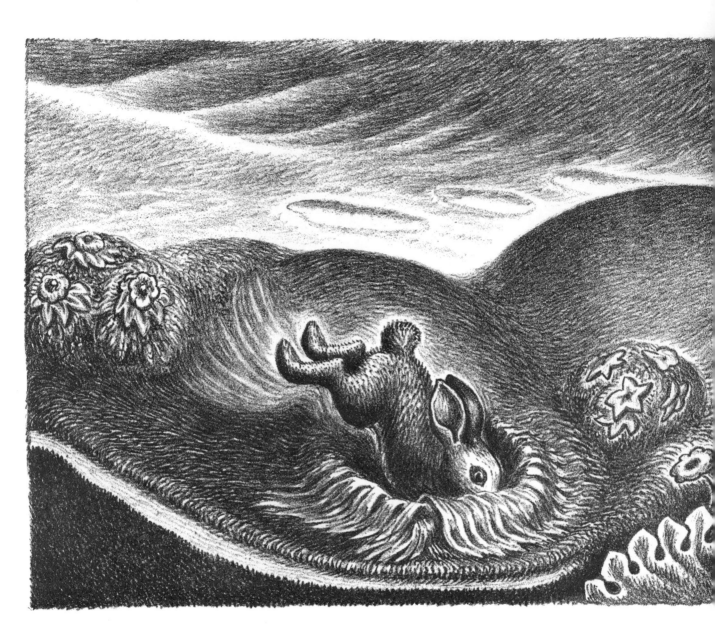

for eXit — off , away !

That's enough for us today

for You , take one last loo

 for Zero – close the book!

ABC

MUSIC BY FLAVIA GÁG

A for Ap - ple big and red, Tra la la la la la la , *B* for Bun - ny
F for Frog - he's fat and funny, Tra la la la la la la , "Looks like rain," say

snug a-bed, Tra la la la la la la, *C* for Crash! *D* for Dash! *E* for Elsewhere
he to Bun-ny, Tra la la la la la la, *G* for Gale! *H* for Hail! Hip-py hop goes

rit.

in a flash Tra la la la la la la la, Elsewhere in a flash, tra la. *I* for Insect
Bunny's tail Tra la la la la la la la, Hip-py hip-py hop, tra la.

here and there *J* for Jay with jaunty air *K* for Kitten catnip-crazy *L* for Lizard

Look how lazy! *M* for Mealtime— munch, munch, munch! M-m-m! these greens are good for lun

SONG

N for Napping in a nook, O for Owl with bookish look. P for prickly Porc-u-pine
T for Tripping back to Town

Tra la la la la la la,
Tra la la la la la la,
Pins and needles on his spine, Tra la la la la la la
U for Up and Up-side-down, Tra la la la la la la

Q for Quail, R for Rail, S for Squirrel Swishy-tail, Tra la la la
V for View, Val-ley too, W——— "We welcome you!" Tra la la la

la la la, Squirrel Swishy-tail tra la.
la la la, Welcome you, tra la tra la.
X for eXit— off, away!

That's enough for us to-day, Y for You, take one last look, Z for Zero— close the book!

Wanda Gág (1893–1946) is best known for her Newbery Honor classics *Millions of Cats* and *The ABC Bunny*. Born in New Ulm, Minnesota, the eldest daughter of Bohemian immigrants, she achieved international acclaim as a children's book author, artist, and illustrator. In addition to her work for children, she was an innovative printmaker and an influential member of the vibrant New York art community in the 1920s and 1930s. Her books *The ABC Bunny, The Funny Thing, Gone Is Gone, or the Story of a Man Who Wanted to Do Housework, Nothing at All, Snippy and Snappy,* and *Snow White and the Seven Dwarfs* are all available from the University of Minnesota Press.

JUN 2 9 2005

WITHDRAWN